T0068086

Angel Scents

Karen Basye

Order this book online at www.trafford.com
or email orders@trafford.com

Most Trafford titles are also available at major online book retailers.

Printed in the United States of America.

ISBN: 978-1-4669-1156-7 (sc)
ISBN: 978-1-4669-1157-4 (e)

Library of Congress Control Number: 2012900545

Trafford rev. 01/16/2012

 www.trafford.com

North America & international
toll-free: 1 888 232 4444 (USA & Canada)
phone: 250 383 6864 ♦ fax: 812 355 4082

Occasionally, you will meet someone whom will claim to have experienced an encounter with a spirit or ghost. Some believe the encounters are merely our minds playing tricks on us. This book is based on true life experiences with some being fiction and some non-fiction. How do we know when and if our experiences are real? After reading the story, you can decide.

The year 1993 a beautiful baby girl was born. There were no cries heard in the delivery room except for the mothers, when the physician said "It's A Girl." The silence was deafening. "Is she alright?" the mother asked. The doctor then placed the baby in the mother's arms. With fear in her eyes, she nestled the baby in her arms. While adoring the beauty of this curly, brown hair, blue eyed baby, she noticed the baby girl staring into her eyes. This glowing beauty she was holding had her mesmerized. "She's like an angel." The mother stated in a soft soothing voice. The baby had a sparkle in her eyes which shone like a star from heaven in the midnight sky. The mother knew at that moment, this baby would be very special in some way.

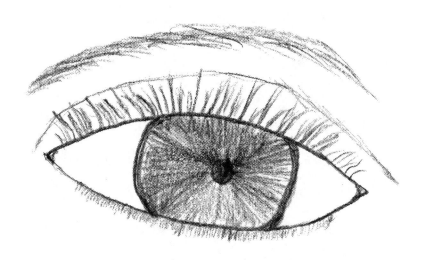

As the months went by, the baby grew more beautiful than ever. She had a smile that would light up a dark room. At the age of six months, the baby became ill. She was diagnosed with Leukemia. She fought a hard battle for a year and a half, but the disease was too advanced for her to fight. Shortly after her second birthday she went to heaven. While in her mothers arms the baby placed her cold hand on her mothers cheek as she stared into her eyes. The sparkle in her eyes became very bright. There was a sweet smell, the essence of a sugar cookie that came over her. It was at that moment mom knew her little angel would always be with her. Over the years mom had noticed the sweet smell around her, especially during trying times.

This is how I find comfort.

In the dawn of a new day, two brothers, ages six and ten arose from their beds. The sun shining through their windows alarmed them of the good weather ahead for their camping trip. They quickly ran down the hall into their parent's bedroom. The boys were jumping up and down shouting, "Let's go camping, it's a great day." After arousing their parents, they ran back to their rooms, they grabbed their camping clothes and threw them into the bags. Running down the stairs, clothes hanging out all over, they were yelling "Let's go let's go!" The boys quickly jumped into the back seat of the SUV. Meanwhile mom and dad gathered the rest of the gear. The back of the car was filled with a tent, camping gear and groceries. The top was covered with a canoe and fishing gear. The family headed out for a great adventure in the mountains.

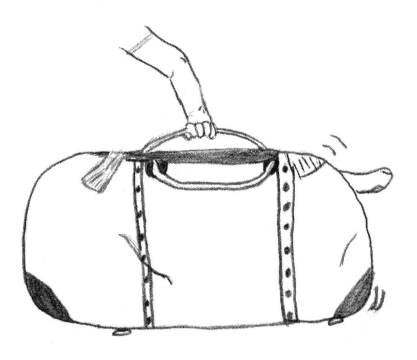

When the family arrived at their campsite, mom and dad explained the dangers of the wilderness to the boys. The ten year old, Chris listened attentively, while David, the six year old, fidgeted. David was too eager to begin fishing to listen to rules. Once the camp was set up they all went for a hike in the woods. While hiking, Dad explained the importance of staying on the trails. "These woods are full of wild animals. You must be cautious." With a firm voice mom added, "We must stay together at all times." Once they reached the bottom of the hill, they found a flat area at the rivers edge. This area of the river was calm. It made a great place for them to fish and swim. There were big rocks to climb on and little rocks to skip in the water. They got the canoe and put it in the water. Dad tied a rope to the canoe and the other end to a sturdy tree on shore. This was so they could float out to the middle of the river to fish and pull themselves back to shore. Once they caught enough fish for dinner, dad pulled them back to shore. "Look at the beautiful sunset." said mom. The sky was glowing with red, orange and yellow beams of light gleaming through the trees. "Let's head back to camp. It will be dark soon" Explained dad. They walked the same path back to camp as they followed to the river.

After arriving back at camp, dad started a fire so mom could cook the fish. The sky was clear and the stars shone so bright, as if there were nightlights on in the sky. With full belly's, they sang a few camp songs and became very tired. Chris and David crawled into their tents. David was so tired he fell fast asleep. Chris on the other hand had trouble falling asleep. While listening to all the strange noises of the wilderness, Chris chanted; "Now I lay me down to sleep, bears don't eat me or I'll scream." Mom and dad were finally able to sleep.

As day began to break, David awoke. Stretching and rubbing his eyes, it dawned on him they were camping. David quickly crawled out of his tent and stood outside gazing at the vast amount of trees around him. A slight breeze was blowing, causing the trees to lose their leaves. Since everyone was still asleep, David decided to collect the colorful leaves as they fell. Shoving them into his pockets as he was walking, he paid no attention to his whereabouts. Reaching for a bright red leaf as it fell toward him; David came too close to the hills edge and slipped. David tumbled to the bottom. Unhurt he stood up, brushed himself off and looked back at the hill. Wow did I fall down the mountain? He muttered to himself.

The breeze became a little stronger causing the leaves to fall by the hundreds. Gazing around, David realized he had landed at the river where they left the canoe. Continuing his leaf hunt David watched a huge colorful leaf fall. It was out of his reach. The leaf had landed in the water behind the canoe. He carefully climbed into the canoe and slowly moved to the back where he could reach the leaf. David held the leaf up so to examine it and let the water drip off it. The wind began to blow harder causing leaves to fall faster. Satisfied with his collection, David decided to go back to camp and share them with his family. As he climbed to the front of the canoe David noticed the wind had blown the canoe out to the middle of the river. Frantically, he began pulling the rope to get back to shore. Pulling as hard and as fast as he could David made no headway. The other end of the rope suddenly came into his hands. The rope had come untied at the tree allowing David and the canoe to float further downstream.

Meanwhile, back at camp Mom and Dad awoke. Mom started the campfire and straightened up the campsite quietly, so not to wake up the boys. Dad headed to the river to catch more fish for breakfast. When he reached the river, he noticed the canoe was gone. Dad looked downstream, seeing no signs of the canoe. He decided to fish off the shore and look for it later. Dad was sure they would find it later. After catching enough fish for breakfast, dad headed back to the camp. Mom went to the tent to awaken the boys. Poking her head into the tent, she saw Chris looking back at her. She looked over towards David, startled she cried out "Where's David?" Chris quickly searched the pile of bedding where David had slept. Not finding David, Chris scurried out of the tent. Chris and Mom called out to David over and over, while looking around at the vast amount of woods surrounding them.

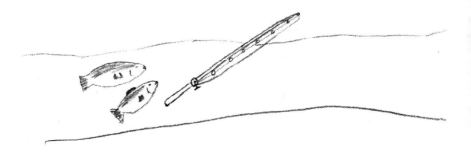

Dad sensed the panic in their voices; he dropped his fish pole and all the fish he had caught and ran all the way back to them. "What's wrong?" dad asked. Mom said in a panic "I can't find David." "He can't be far; It's not been light very long" replied dad. Suddenly chills ran through his body. "The canoe, it was gone!" Thought dad. "Footprints dad; Let's look for his footprints" added Chris.

Unfortunately the leaves covered the ground so there were no footprints to follow. Quickly they all ran to the river. While running and looking around they called for David. There were no replies, and when they reached the river, there still was no sign of David or the canoe.

Mom ran to the Parks Ranger station to summon for help, while Dad and Chris continued their search. They followed the river downstream calling out to David and searching for the canoe. Hearing no replies, and seeing no sign of the canoe they quickly ran on further. The park Rangers told mom to stay at the camp in case David returned.

Meanwhile David enjoyed the leisure ride down the river without a care in the world. The wind began to blow harder, causing the river to move at a more rapid pace. The further down the river he went, the more rocks there were. The canoe started hitting the rocks and bouncing off them, tossing David around. David was too scared to make a noise so he held on as tight as he could, and rode the rapids. There was a narrowing in the river with trees hanging over the rocks. The river was getting louder and the water was more rapid splashing off the rocks. David thought this was the end of the river because he couldn't see water past the tree branches. David was so excited; he stood up with his arms in the air he shouted "Hooray I made it to the end!" Suddenly he was grabbed in the middle of his stomach by a tree branch. His body wrapped around the branch as if he were hugging it. The canoe was tossed around in the rapids until it disappeared into the falls. Suspended over the rapids, David was afraid to let go in fear he would disappear too. Forgetting about the canoe, David climbed the branch as quickly as he could to get to shore. He wanted to be as far from the water as he could get. Finally he reached shore, sat down, and gathered his thoughts. "I better get back to camp" he thought to himself. David found the trail and headed back to camp. So he thought. He was on the opposite side of the river and headed deeper into the forest.

Dad and Chris continued their search. As they reached the rapids, dad gulped in fear of what he might find. They quickly ran down the hill to the bottom of the falls. Suddenly, dad dropped to his knees when all he saw was a broken canoe resting on the rocks below. "Please! God let David be safe!" he pleaded. There was no sign of David. They continued their search in fear of the worst.

David kept walking until his little legs were too tired to carry him any further. He sat down next to a blackberry bush. He picked a berry and ate it and then another and another. He soon was picking them with both hands simultaneously and shoving them into his mouth. Feeling full and sleepy, David decided to lie down. He fell fast asleep.

Back at the river, Dad and Chris continued their search and calling for David. Dad was lost in his thoughts and confused of where to look or what to do. "Please Lord bring David back to us and keep him safe from harm." He prayed. Soon after they headed back to camp with hopes that David had returned. Mom heard footsteps from the path, quickly she stood up and called out "David" but it wasn't him. Dad said "sorry" hanging his head down. They all embraced in silence. The rangers continued searching while mom and dad kept the fire going; hoping David would see it and find his way back.

The sun had set and the moon was full. Chris was exhausted. He sat in front of his tent and prayed. "Dear Lord, Please send an angel to be with David to keep him safe from the wild animals and bring him back to us". Mom helped Chris into his tent and as she covered him she said, "We will find him, we will." Mom sat on a rock near the fire. "Lord, please bring my baby back. Let him cry so I can hear him." She prayed. With a small brush of wind mom could smell a sweet scent. It gave her chills. She stood up, looked around and said, "Baby girl go to David, keep him safe and bring him back to us." The sweet scent instantly vanished. Mom then, sure of her thoughts, rested her head on a rock and drifted off to sleep.

Dad sat by the fire listening and waiting for a word from the rangers. As dad sat he watched the lights from the helicopters as they continued the search. Dad didn't mention the broken canoe to mom, but that was all that was going through his mind. Restless, he decided to go search some more. He grabbed a flashlight and headed down river again.

The next morning the sun began to rise. Still asleep beside the blackberry bush David was startled awake by something cold on his cheek. He jumped up, looked around but saw nothing. David realized he was lost and began crying. Suddenly he heard someone coming. "Mom, Dad, is that you?" he called out. There was no answer. He could see movement in the trees. He then realizes it wasn't his parents. It was a big black bear. Quickly he crawled under the blackberry bush. Lying as still as he could, taking slow deep breaths, David watched the bear get closer and closer. The bear reached the bush sniffing and snorting while eating the berries. David trembled in fear of being eaten.

Suddenly a bright beam of light shined through the trees directly into the bear's eyes. Irritated, the bear grumbled and ran off. When the bear was out of sight, David slowly crawled out from under the bush. He followed another path and hoped it was the right one.

Hunger came over him again but he thought, "I am not going near another blackberry bush again." A breeze began to blow. David thought he could smell mom baking cookies. With excitement, he began running and calling out, "Mom, Mom!"

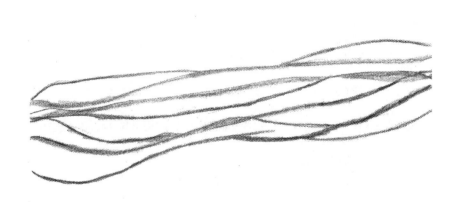

Dad was at the river still searching when he heard a little voice. Listening carefully, he realized it was David. Quickly looking back and forth from side to side calling out "David?" "Dad is that you?" replied David. Finally they saw each other from across the river. Fearlessly dad jumped in and swam to the other side. He grabbed David embraced him and cried. "I am so happy to see you. Thank you Lord. Thank you." Dad said out loud. He carried David across the river and all the way back to camp.

Approaching camp, Dad calls out "I found him, David is safe." Mom and Chris ran to greet them. They all embraced with tears of joy. David innocently perked up and asked "where's the cookies mom?" Mom then knew it was her little angel that brought David back.

The search was called off and the family went home.

A few weeks went by when mom and dad asked the boys if they would like to go camping again. Chris' eyes opened wide as he uttered "what? Are you out of your minds?" He walked away shaking his head from side to side. David on the other hand was eager for another adventure.

The next morning as the sun peaked through the windows waking David, he jumped up, woke up Chris and ran to mom and dads room shouting "Let's go let's go." Mom and dad got up and collected all their gear. "Come on Chris." Mom called. As Chris walked down the hall he grumbled, "I cannot believe after all we went through, you all still want to camp. But ok if you say so." Regrettably he walked to the car.

"What's going on? Great! We don't even leave the driveway and they are all missing." "Chris we're back here." called Dad. He went to the back yard and there he found the whole family. The tents were pitched and there was a little campfire. "All right!" shouted Chris.

Mom looked up at the sunlight gleaming through the trees. They all enjoyed the breeze as it blew a sweet scent all around them.

I once again could cherish the moment with my entire family.

Dear Reader,

Please use the following pages to write about events in your life. There are no rules. Just write. I found it easy to clear my mind by writing my feelings down. I am not good about sharing my feelings verbally, so writing them down is my alternative. If you are comfortable, share with others. You never know how this may help. I have found this to be a great part of my healing process. I pray you will find yours.

Sincerely,

Karen

What event took place so dear to my heart?

_____

_____

_____

_____

_____

_____

_____

_____

_____

_____

_____

_____

_____

_____

How am I handling my situation?

_____

_____

_____

_____

_____

_____

_____

_____

_____

_____

_____

_____

_____

_____

_____

How should I respond?

_____

_____

_____

_____

_____

_____

_____

_____

_____

_____

_____

_____

_____

Why am I grieving?

_____

_____

_____

_____

_____

_____

_____

_____

_____

_____

_____

_____

_____

_____

_____

Did I remember to ask God to take my pain, because I need a break?

Do I have a good friend and/or a family member I can share my feelings with? In your community, there are support groups as well. Remember people don't usually like to bring up a conversation about what hurts you because they don't know what to say. Others are sometimes afraid to talk about what hurts you because they don't want to bring up thoughts which might upset you. Let them know how you feel. I sometimes am alright talking about my daughter and sometimes it upsets me too much to talk about her.

I just tell them I just don't want to discuss this at this time.

I have never offended anyone with my reply.

Please remember, you are not alone. There is someone out there wanting to share your story. It does not have to be a book. Just open your heart and let it out. Who would you like to share your heart with?

_____

_____

_____

_____

_____

_____

_____

_____

_____

_____

_____

Am I able to heal the way I am handling my situation?

_____

_____

_____

_____

_____

_____

_____

_____

_____

_____

_____

_____

Dear Reader,

I Hope my book has helped in some way. It has helped me to write my story. Thank you for listening. I would love to hear from you and if my book has helped you in any way. Please feel free to share your story with me. You may write to me and send it to…

Karen Basye

498 Widewater rd

Stafford, Va. 22554

Sincerely and God bless you,

Karen Basye